SCARY HOWL OF FAME

By Sheryl Scarborough and Sharon McCoy
Illustrated by Dianne O'Quinn Burke

Sterling Publishing Company, Inc.
New York

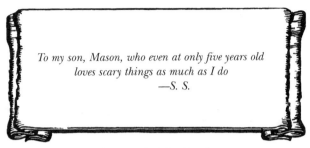

To my son, Mason, who even at only five years old
loves scary things as much as I do
—S. S.

Library of Congress Cataloging-in-Publication Data

Scarborough, Sheryl.
    Scary howl of fame / By Sheryl Scarborough and Sharon McCoy :
    illustrations by Dianne O'Quinn Burke.
        p.   cm.
    Includes index.
    ISBN 0-8069-1312-6 (trade). — ISBN 0-8069-1313-4 (paper)
    1. Monsters—Juvenile literature. 2. Ghosts—Juvenile literature.
I. McCoy, Sharon. II. Burke, Dianne O'Quinn. III. Title.
GR825.S29   1995
001.9'44—dc20   94-49530
                                                               CIP
10 9 8 7 6 5 4 3 2 1   AC

Cover illustration: Will Suckow
Design and layout: Frank Loose Design, Portland, Oregon

Published by Sterling Publishing Company, Inc.
387 Park Avenue South, New York, NY 10016
© 1995 by RGA Publishing Group, Inc.
Illustrations © 1995 by Dianne O'Quinn Burke
Distributed in Canada by Sterling Publishing
℅ Canadian Manda Group, One Atlantic Avenue, Suite 105
Toronto, Ontario, Canada M6K 3E7
Distributed in Great Britain and Europe by Cassell PLC
Wellington House, 125 Strand, London WC2R 0BB, England
Distributed in Australia by Capricorn Link (Australia) Pty Ltd.
P.O. Box 6651, Baulkham Hills, Business Centre,
NSW 2153, Australia

Sterling ISBN 0-8069-1312-6 (Trade)
                0-8069-1313-4 (Paper)

CONTENTS

INTRODUCTION

The Omen

Our world is full of scary things, both real and imagined. *The Scary Howl of Fame* celebrates them all, offering you the scariest of the scary, the best of beasts, the chilliest thrillers, and the ghastliest ghouls!

As you savor each *Howl of Fame* entry, try not to count the goose bumps spreading along

your arms and creeping up the back of your neck. A sweater might chase the chill from your room, but will it protect you from the tattletale tombstone?

Is that creaking door just your imagination, or are you suddenly no longer alone? Maybe that scraping sound you hear is just the wind blowing the trees and not the unkillable mega-movie-star slasher Jason, lurking outside.

If you find yourself starting to freak out, sweat pouring from your brow, take a deep breath, pick up the phone, and dial a friend.

Your friend's not home? You can always go to sleep. Just try real hard not to think about vampire bats or black widow spiders—or any of the other creepy, crawly things that could silently sneak up under the covers in search of your warm flesh and blood.

Can't sleep? Then read on. This book may not scare you to death, but it will give you a new look at the most chilling, sinister slices of the scariest tidbits on earth!

Chapter 1

GHASTLY GHOSTS

Why ghosts exist has never been adequately explained, and many people *say* they don't believe in them. Nonetheless, strange thumps and bangs, transparent figures floating through walls, and shrieks that break the sound barrier scare the living daylights out of all of us! What you are about to read are among the creepiest, scariest, and most bizarre ghastly ghost tales ever recorded.

THE CREEPIEST CONFESSION

Padre Lecuona, Mexico City

In the early 1800s, an unsuspecting Mexican priest heard a dreadful confession . . . from a dead man. The encounter, which occurred in Mexico City, proved to be the most tormenting experience of the priest's life and went down in history as one of the creepiest confessions ever told.

One stormy winter evening, Padre Lecuona hurried through the stinging rain to the house of a friend. On his way he heard the voice of an old woman call out to him: "Padre, please wait. You must hear a confession. It is urgent,

7

we haven't a moment to lose!" The priest, eager to arrive at his destination, answered, "Surely one of the other priests can attend to this matter."

"Oh no," declared the woman. "He asks for you—and only you!"

The woman led the padre to a dilapidated, darkened house in an alley. As he followed her through the door, a wave of foul air assaulted him. The woman lit a candle. In the flickering glow, he could see the form of an emaciated man lying flat on his back on the floor in the corner. As the priest knelt down, he sensed something was wrong. The man's skin was brown and leathery, stretched tightly over bones. The head was but a skull scarcely covered with skin and a few wisps of matted hair. "Mother of God!" gasped Padre Lecuona. "This is no living man!"

Suddenly, the figure rose to a sitting position and croaked, "Forgive me, Father, for I have sinned." In a raspy voice, the corpse recounted how, years before, a gang of thieves had broken into his home, stolen all of his possessions, and murdered him and his wife with a hunting knife.

CLAIM TO FRIGHT FAME

The house where the supernatural confession took place sat in an alley in Mexico City. Soon after the padre died, the townspeople dedicated the alley to the priest by naming it Callejón del Padre Lecuona (meaning the Alley of Father Lecuona), which it is still called today. It is said to be a dark and dangerous place, haunted by evil spirits.

Because he died so quickly, he was never able to receive his last rites by a priest. Now, he claimed, through divine intervention, he had been permitted to return and make his confession.

Horrified at what he was seeing and hearing, the priest quickly forgave the man for the sins in his previous life. When he was finished, the man crumpled into a mummified corpse. The priest fled the house at once and began looking for the old woman in hopes of getting an explanation for the bizarre occurrence, but she had disappeared.

The next day, still in shock, Padre Lecuona and a friend returned to the house in the alley. The door looked as if it had not been opened in years. Cobwebs stretched over it, even over the rusted keyhole. Could the entire incident have been a dream? Distraught, the men broke into the house. Inside they saw only a vacant room. "Hello?" the men called, but their voices echoed through the empty house. As Padre Lecuona turned to leave, he saw a handkerchief lying in the corner where the corpse had been. It was the one he had in his possession the night before. As he bent to pick it up, a sharp pain shot through his chest, and a wave of dizziness engulfed him.

"Are you all right?" the priest's friend asked in alarm.

"I think so," answered the padre, but those were the last words he ever spoke. The priest clawed at the door, opened it, and then stumbled out into the alley. Three days later, after lapsing into a state of delirium, the padre died. Doctors were never able to find a cause or reason for his tragic demise, but when the house was demolished years later, a mouldy, crumpled, mummified skeleton (the corpse who confessed?) was found behind one of the walls.

THE MOST MENACING MESSAGE FROM THE GRAVE

Schultz Family Tombstone, Cherokee County, Iowa

Eerie things are sighted in graveyards, but few of them remain in place for all the world to see. A heinous crime, which occurred in Washta, Iowa, in Cherokee County at the turn of the 20th century, was followed by one of the most ominous sights ever seen on a tombstone!

Heinrich and Olga Schultz, husband and wife, were a kind, elderly couple who lived on a small farm in Iowa. They were well liked, having no enemies. In fact, neighbors and townspeople all respected and admired the Schultzes because of their honest nature and willingness to help other people.

Therefore, it was a sickening shock when, in the middle of a frigid winter night, they were murdered in cold blood. Their bodies were found in their home— their heads split open with an ax! There were signs every- where of a struggle: Heinrich and Olga fought hard to save their lives, but unfortunately

lost the battle. When the townspeople heard the news of their brutal deaths, they shivered with outrage . . . and fear.

Three days before his death, Heinrich had withdrawn his life savings from the bank, feeling it would be safer at home. When the bodies were found, the money was gone—along with the Schultzes' hired hand and boarder, Will Florence. Everyone, including the authorities, was convinced that Will had murdered the couple and stolen the money. Will had always been a troublemaker, but Heinrich felt the need to give him a chance by offering him work around the farm.

An aggressive manhunt ensued, and Will was finally found hiding out in Nebraska. The police couldn't get their hands on enough physical evidence to convict him of the murders, so he was released.

In the weeks to come, a strange phenomenon began to unfold at the graveyard where the Schultzes were buried. A face began to appear in the marble of the joint headstone that the couple shared. Over the course of three or four weeks, the picture grew clearer and clearer. Just as film under chemical action develops a negative, the marble tombstone developed the picture of a face. Rumor of this event circulated, and eventually, law-enforcement officials visited the graveyard. Even the most skeptical detectives gasped in shock when they saw it. The perfect likeness of Will Florence was etched into the tombstone.

Several months later, new evidence implicating Will Florence as the murderer surfaced, but although an enormous search took place, he was never found. To this day, though, his guilt remains stamped upon the marble tombstone atop the Schultzes' graves, which still stands today in Cherokee County.

Runner-Up: Harriet's Threat from the Grave

Henry and Harriet lived in Kirksville, Missouri, and had been married for thirty years when Harriet became ill in the winter of 1873 and died suddenly. The couple had been happy together, with only occasional arguments due to Harriet's jealousy over other women. Soon after Harriet died, Henry married a younger woman.

Immediately after the wedding, mysterious things started happening. Rocks would fall from the sky and come crashing down on their house; during the night, blankets would mysteriously fly off the bed, and the pillows would disappear. For weeks the newlyweds were tormented by eerie events.

Then came the night Henry would never forget. Unable to sleep, he was in bed reading. His wife dozed silently beside him. Suddenly, an invisible hand rolled back the blankets to reveal a handwritten message on the sheet: "These things shall continue forever!" With a chill, Henry recognized the handwriting. Harriet, his first wife, had delivered a warning from the grave. Whether or not she held to her threat is unknown.

THE MOST FAMOUS GHOST

The Ghost of Christmas Future from *A Christmas Carol*

In 1843, Charles Dickens wrote one of the most famous and widely read ghost stories of all time, *A Christmas Carol*. In the tale, Dickens introduces Ebenezer Scrooge, a mean-spirited and selfish old man who, on one dark and stormy night, meets up with three spirits, the Ghosts of Christmas Past, Present, and Yet to Come. It is the intention of these ghosts to try to change the course of the evil man's life.

By far the scariest and most menacing phantom that visits Scrooge on that fateful night is the Ghost of Christmas Yet to Come.

Dressed in a deep black garment that entirely conceals his head and body, the ghost displays to Scrooge only one outstretched, bony hand. The dreaded spirit goes on to show Scrooge his dismal future . . . a lonely, unadorned grave with Scrooge's own name engraved on the stone.

Charles Dickens's very first public reading was of *A Christmas Carol.* Spectators say he gave such a spine-chilling account of the Ghost of Christmas Yet to Come, he had the entire audience trembling with fear and excitement. That one evening's reading committed Dickens to the career of touring around and reading his stories in public. Dickens actually earned more money as a public reader than he ever did from the sale of his books.

Runners-Up: Top Four Famous Ghosts

1. **Nelly Butler's ghost:** During the early 1800s, Nelly, the former wife of a famous captain, George Butler, appeared as a spirit to over one hundred people. She supposedly haunted her husband's home to ensure that he marry a young woman by the name of Lydia Blaisdel. Nelly's spirit told the captain to treat Lydia in a loving manner because she would die in childbirth before a year had passed. Both the marriage and Lydia's death occurred within the year.

2. **James Chaffin's ghost:** James Chaffin of North Carolina died in 1921 and was survived by his wife and several sons. However, his will decreed that only one son would inherit his fortune. One night in 1925, the ghost of James appeared to two of his sons and told them this: "Read

Genesis, chapter 27, in my daddy's old Bible." With several witnesses, the sons found and opened the Bible to Genesis. Tucked between the pages was a will written in their father's writing that instructed the property be equally divided among the entire family. The state of North Carolina recognized it as legal and invalidated the first will.

3. **Abraham Lincoln's ghost:** Abraham Lincoln, the sixteenth president of the United States, has been sighted as a ghostly apparition many times. Lincoln's ghost was first reported by Grace Coolidge, the wife of Calvin Coolidge, the thirtieth president. She observed Lincoln's tall figure staring out of a window in the Oval Office. After that, Lincoln's apparition was also seen many times during Franklin Delano Roosevelt's presidency. Some people believe that Lincoln was a psychic and had foreseen his own death in several dreams.

4. **Anne Boleyn's ghost:** Anne was the second and best known of the six wives of King Henry VIII. The King, eager to divorce Anne soon after they were married, had Anne imprisoned in the Tower of London and beheaded. Anne Boleyn's ghost has been sighted many times in the Tower, with and without her head. Witnesses often report that they see a woman in white drift out of a room in the Tower and float towards them.

THE MOST GRUESOME PIRATE GHOST

Blackbeard the Pirate

The pirates of old were legendary, larger-than-life men who
lived at sea on ships that they often stole from innocent
people trying to make their way to new lands. Few pirates
were more feared than Edward Teach, otherwise known as
Blackbeard the Pirate. The captain of his own ship,
Blackbeard punished his men harshly and didn't hesitate
to shoot or throw overboard a disobedient sailor.

His murderous, plundering wild life caught up with him
in 1718 when Lieutenant Robert Maynard of England's Royal
Navy surprised Blackbeard at the pirate's favorite cove,
Ocracoke Inlet, off the Gulf of Mexico.

Maynard and his men laid a trap, and the
evil Blackbeard sailed right into it. Within
minutes, Maynard and Blackbeard were
duelling hand-to-hand in a fierce
sword fight. The hulking
Blackbeard snapped
Maynard's sword in half,
leaving him helpless.
When he raised his
cutlass to finish
Maynard off, one
of Maynard's men
snuck up from
behind Blackbeard
and cut his throat.

Legend has
it that even
while blood
was spurting from
his neck, Blackbeard

16

kept fighting. It took an additional five shots and twenty stab wounds to finally lay him to rest. Fearing the ferocious pirate might possibly come back to life, Maynard had Blackbeard's head cut off and hung from the ship's bow. The sailors said that when Blackbeard's body was dumped into the ocean, the head cried out for it and the body swam around the ship three times before sinking.

Ever since, Blackbeard's ghost has haunted the area of his bloody death. Fishermen have reported an eerie, glowing, headless body floating just below the surface of the ocean. And sometimes, around Ocracoke Inlet, Blackbeard's ghost ventures ashore in search of his head!

CLAIM TO FRIGHT FAME

So what happened to Blackbeard's severed head? After it hung from the bow of Maynard's ship, the head was taken apart. Blackbeard's skull was then coated with silver and used as a most grotesque punch bowl.

THE MOST ABSURD GHOST

The Creepy Chicken of Pond Square, England

Don't laugh too fast. A chicken may not sound scary, but what if it were the *ghost* of a chicken, gruesomely killed as part of a scientific experiment?

This ghastly ghost dates back to the 1600s—a time before people knew much about how things live, before DNA tests and test-tube babies and heart transplants. People who conducted scientific experiments often dug up graves to study the bodies of dead people. This activity, and the knowledge that came from it, were both startling and frightening to "normal, decent folks," who felt one shouldn't question why people live and breathe.

Back in 1626, scientist and philosopher Sir Francis Bacon observed that grass appeared to die when covered by a thick blanket of snow, but would come back to life when the snow melted and spring began. As a scientist, he wondered— would an animal also die if it were surrounded by snow, but then live again shortly thereafter? In order to find out,

Bacon killed a chicken, ripped out its organs, and stuffed it with snow.

Lord Bacon never had the opportunity to find out whether or not the chicken would come back to life. Handling the snow gave Bacon a chill. He took very ill and died a few days later. Strangely, the body of the chicken disappeared from the scene without any explanation.

While Lord Bacon's ghost has never been sighted, the creepy chicken's bizarre little spirit has. There have been hundreds of accounts by witnesses throughout the ages about a mysterious chicken in Pond Square, England, the site where the chicken was murdered, feebly hopping and flying in circles, and then disappearing right before witnesses' eyes!

THE BLACK SPANIELS OF BALLECHIN HOUSE, IN PERTHSHIRE, SCOTLAND

When Major Stewart of Ballechin House died in 1876, his relatives didn't want to bother finding homes for his prized pets. Instead, they had his fourteen black spaniels destroyed. Ever since that time, residents and visitors to the house have reported hearing people arguing, and dogs barking and whining. They've also felt invisible dogs sniffing and pushing at them. Some have even seen one of the spaniels appear and disappear. One woman saw paws resting on a table— but no dog's body was connected to them!

STRANGEST GHOSTLY VEHICLE

The Big Red Bus of Ladbroke Grove, England

It's one thing to experience the ghost of a person, or even a chicken or a dog. They were at least *once* living, breathing beings. But how would you feel if confronted by a large, inanimate object that has suddenly taken on a life all its own?

In Ladbroke Grove, England, a phantom red bus caused horrific accidents and unexplainable deaths during the 1930s.

Hundreds of drivers told police that as they turned a certain corner, a giant, double-decker red bus would suddenly appear, speeding straight towards them. As if this weren't bad enough, the bus had no driver! Its inside lights were brightly lit, and its approaching headlights blinded terrified motorists!

The drivers would be so startled by the oncoming ghostly bus that they'd yank their steering wheels to the right or left to get out of the way. Several people ran their cars up onto the sidewalks on the left or crashed into the dividers on the right. Many of these accidents ended in death.

The bus, so enormous and scary—and so seemingly real—would disappear as soon as it turned the corner towards the Ladbroke Grove bus station.

Finally, in the mid-1930s, the British government had the road straightened in hopes of diminishing the number of accidents. It didn't stop every car crash on that stretch, but the big red phantom bus was never seen again!

Runner-Up: The Ghost Ship *Palatine*

Two hundred years ago, the crew of the ship *Palatine* rebelled against their captain and killed him when food and water ran low. The crew forced some of the passengers to pay for their food. Others were murdered and thrown overboard.

The crew of the *Palatine* beached the ship on remote Block Island in the Atlantic Ocean. There they stripped the ship of anything valuable that remained, set it on fire, and allowed it to drift out to sea. To this day, people say that the *Palatine* appears, glowing brightly in the fog, on the Saturday between Christmas and New Year's—the very day on which she was burned.

MOST HAUNTING HITCHHIKER

Resurrection Mary

It began one fateful night when a beautiful, young blond girl who loved to dance was tragically killed in a car accident on her way home from the O. Henry Ballroom in the 1930s. She was buried in Chicago's Resurrection Cemetery.

Apparently, her love of dancing was not diminished by death. Even to this day, drivers along the stretch of road where Resurrection Cemetery is located report being flagged down by a beautiful young girl dressed in a ball gown from the 1930s and dancing shoes. They call her Resurrection Mary.

When drivers stop to give a ride to the mysterious hitch-hiker, sometimes she asks to be dropped off at the ballroom, which still stands, and is now called the Willowbrook Ballroom, and other times she asks for a ride home. They

report that as they approach the ancient iron gates of the cemetery, their mysterious passenger either asks them to stop or else vanishes before their eyes. At least one gentleman has reported receiving a kiss from the young lady before she departed.

CLAIM TO FRIGHT FAME

Stories of vanishing hitchhikers seem to be gaining in popularity as hundreds of sightings are reported worldwide. Researchers Richard Beardsley and Rosemary Hankey analyzed nearly 80 cases of phantom hitchhikers in the United States, for the *California Folklore Quarterly*, some years ago. Beardsley and Hankey decided the cases fell into three distinct categories.

Half the sightings involved ghostly hitchhikers who gave an address to the driver before disappearing. The perplexed driver would go to the address seeking an answer to the disappearance and would find out their hitchhiker actually died years before.

The next two categories involve women, either young or old, who approach male drivers. These female phantoms ask to borrow a scarf or coat before vanishing. The article of clothing is later found on a grave.

The last type of ghostly hitchhiker is found only in Hawaii and is identified as a local goddess. Pele, the guardian of Hawaii's largest volcano, Mauna Loa, is reportedly a frequent phantom hitchhiker who disappears not long after gaining entrance to the car. However, according to legend, Pele is very bad tempered, and it is bad luck to refuse to give her a ride.

Chapter 2

MONSTERS WITH THE MOST

Hideous, cruel, and murderous monsters are found in books, movies, and on television. Many of them are so lifelike you could swear they're real! Because monsters are filled with so much hate, you never know what to expect from them. Often, revenge is their favorite pastime—usually resulting in brutal and bloody deaths.

THE SLASHER WHO WON'T DIE

Jason

What famous movie monster has defied death and destruction more than any other character? Jason, the mad slasher from the horror film series *Friday the 13th,* wins this category hands down!

In the original *Friday the 13th,* an entire summer camp staff was slaughtered by a demented mother whose son had been allowed to drown by incompetent camp counselors. At the end of the film, the sick woman is killed by one remaining counselor. The stage is now set for Jason to come back and wreak vengeance on the killer of his mother and all other camp counselors . . . again . . . and again . . . and again. So far, he has come back nine times in nine different movies, and there's a rumor that a total of thirteen Jason movies are planned.

In every *Friday the 13th* movie, Jason "dies" a grotesque death. Ready for the details?

Friday the 13th (**1980**): Jason gets his head cut off with a machete.

Friday the 13th, Part 2 (**1981**): A machete lands deep in his torso.

Friday the 13th, Part 3 (**1982**): Jason gets an axe slashed through his head.

Friday the 13th, The Final Chapter (**1984**): Again, Jason gets his head whacked with a machete, splitting his skull down the middle.

Friday the 13th, Part V (**1985**): Jason falls on the steel-spiked teeth of a tractor harrow (although it turns out that it wasn't Jason who fell, but an imitator who used the Jason legend so that he could kill kids).

Friday the 13th, Part VI (**1986**): The propeller of an outboard motor slices, chews, and gnaws into the flesh of Jason's neck. He sinks to the bottom of the lake. (But before the final credits, he is clearly seen opening his eyes underwater.)

Friday the 13th, Part VII (**1988**): Jason is chained and thrown to the bottom of the lake (but since the movie opens with an imitator putting on the infamous hockey mask that Jason wears, the viewer isn't sure who really sinks to the bottom and drowns).

Friday the 13th, Part VIII: Jason Takes Manhattan (**1989**): Jason gets toxic waste thrown in his face, which melts it into a grotesque skeleton. Then he is drowned in an underground sewer. A little boy's voice cries out, "Mommy, don't let me drown."

Jason Goes to Hell: The Final Friday (1993): Jason is pulled down into the ground by dozens of clutching, mud-caked hands.

In all nine movies the same basic plot survives with Jason picking off teenagers left and right. Most of the time you'll only see his shoes, hands, or shadow perform the murders, and that adds to the fear. But, by far the scariest thing about Jason is that he *just won't die.* No matter how often he is stabbed, shot, drowned, or bombed, it's a surefire bet that he will be back!

Runner-Up: Freddy Krueger

Scarfaced Freddy Krueger is another monster who kills and kills and kills but never dies himself. In each *Nightmare on Elm Street* movie, he enters teenagers' dreams, and then murders them in bizarre ways. The only way to fend off Freddy is to stay awake . . . forever! With seven movies to his credit, Freddy is close on the heels of Jason.

THE MOST FAMOUS MONSTER

Count Dracula

He stalks the night. His teeth glint in the moonlight, and the dim light reveals razor-sharp fangs—fangs with which he punctures your neck. Then he slowly drinks of the nectar that keeps him alive . . . your blood. This is Count Dracula, the granddaddy of vampires.

Author Bram Stoker created the Count in his celebrated novel *Dracula* (1897). According to Stoker, Dracula was human in form—a tall, old man with white hair and a long, white moustache. He had a long hooked nose, a hard mouth, and sharp white teeth surrounded by red lips. Dracula's stark white complexion was a chilling contrast to the black clothing he always wore.

But did you know that Stoker's inspiration for Count Dracula actually came from

a real, live person? Vlad Dracula V, also known as Vlad the Impaler, became the official prince of Wallachia (now part of Romania) in 1456, when he was barely 25 years old. His bloodthirsty ways were legendary. Vlad treated everyone who displeased him the same way—by impaling them on tall stakes and leaving them hanging in the open air to die slowly. Once his victims were dead, Vlad insisted that the bodies stay in place on the stakes until the flesh rotted off their bones and their joints separated and collapsed.

Vampires of all shapes and sizes have followed in Dracula's teeth-prints, offering up scores of scary stories and images. The most recent interpretation is the character of Lestat from Anne Rice's books, such as *Interview with the Vampire*. Hollywood filmmakers have always had a passion for Dracula and other vampires. There have been more than a hundred vampire movies made, and sixty of those were based on the character of Dracula.

CLAIM TO FRIGHT FAME

Bela Lugosi, a Hungarian-born actor, created the chillingly original character of Dracula in the 1931 movie based on Bram Stoker's novel. At the time of this role, Lugosi spoke very little English. He learned the lines of the movie phonetically, which added to the peculiar speech of the Dracula character in which every word is drawn out and deliberate. Lugosi became so tightly linked with the role of this monster that he was cast as other monsters as well. He became one of Hollywood's favorite horror actors. Tragically, he squandered his fortune on drugs and died, broke and starving. His final request—to be buried in his Dracula cape—was granted.

THE EERIEST WAIL

The Wail of the Banshee

As night falls and fog shrouds the landscape, the stillness is shattered by an eerie moan. The tone is pure agony, a sound that makes your hair stand on end, an inhuman shriek that you will never forget. It is the wail of the banshee.

According to ancient Celtic legend, the mythical banshee is a female elf or fairy who is kind to humans and feels their pain. She will attach herself to certain families, becoming their live-in spirit. Although they can't see her, she is with them every waking moment and while they sleep. She sits and waits, silently, invisibly, for a terrifying event.

When someone in that family dies, the Banshee takes on the pain personally. She wails for them and for all the world

to hear. It is her way of trying to lessen, or at least quicken, the grieving process so the family can get on with things. Her wail can be heard from one county to the next. Her message is always the same: Someone has suffered a loss, someone has passed on.

In the 1700s to 1800s, before radio and television and before daily newspapers were widespread throughout Ireland, England, and parts of Scotland, the main way for a community to find out about a death was to hear the banshee wail. At that point the town would know someone had died. It would then be just a matter of finding out who.

THE EERIEST SOUNDS EVER

- Howl of the werewolf
- Creak of a rusty door hinge
- Crack of shattering glass on a dark night
- Th-thump of your heart pounding in your ears
- Hiss of an angry cat
- Scrape of a tree branch against the window
- Thud of a body hitting the floor
- Rustling in bushes along a dark path
- Moaning wind on a dark and stormy night

THE MOST DREADED GREEK MYTHICAL MONSTER

Medusa

The most terrifying woman of Greek mythology actually got her name because of her never-ending bad hair day. Medusa was considered the queen of the three Gorgons, but she was the only one who was mortal. Gorgons had horrific faces, protruding eyes, and huge serrated teeth. Medusa was both beautiful and hideous, with a classic face that resembled sculpted marble and hair that was literally a teeming mass of writhing, poisonous snakes with sharp fangs pointing off in

all directions. If Medusa did not find someone to her liking, she simply turned him to stone by drawing him into her irresistible hypnotic gaze and forcing her victim to look at her.

Many poor souls fell victim to Medusa's awesome power. But because no one could look at her long enough to kill her, she was nearly unstoppable. A creative solution was devised by the young warrior Perseus. With the help of the goddess Athena, Perseus finally sliced off Medusa's head by using his shield as a mirror and striking backwards, over his shoulder, with his sword.

Medusa's legacy survived, not only in the memory of her petrifying form but in her offspring. As blood poured from her severed neck, Pegasus, the winged horse, literally rose up from the blood and took form.

Medusa's severed head was used to adorn the shield of the god Zeus. But so strong and intense was her evil presence that it was necessary to keep her face veiled—lest her continuing power were to do more damage.

Runner-Up: The Hydra

This giant, nine-headed dragon lived in Lake Lerna in ancient Greece. Wooden sailing ships were reduced to toothpicks by the tail of this huge creature, who seemed to love the taste of humans. Slaying the Hydra was not easy. As soon as one head was cut off, two new ones would grow in its place. Destruction of the Hydra was one of the feats, or labors, performed by Hercules. He solved the problem of multiplying heads by searing the neck with his heated sword after each slice.

THE MOST DEADLY EGYPTIAN MONSTER

The Ouraion

Part serpent, part rooster, this terrifying monster was said to have the head, body, and wings of a bird, with an evil, snake-like tail trailing out behind. Instead of feathers, its entire body was covered with leathery scales. Statues and golden crowns of the Egyptian period were often adorned with the likeness of this hideous creature.

But most frightening was how easily the ouraion could kill. According to Egyptian legends, it had only to breathe on a living being, even without biting it, and the victim would die! One look into the eyes of an ouraion would turn a living thing to dust.

The breath of the ouraion was so toxic it could scorch grass and burst rock. Its poison was almost impossible to avoid. A Greek legend states that an ouraion—or basilisk, as the Greeks called it—was once killed with a spear by a man on horseback. But it was a bitter victory: The poison raced up the spear and killed not only the man but his horse as well, dropping them in their tracks.

Many soldiers encountered this creature in the desert, and though they lived to tell its evil tale, they paid a hefty price. If infected on the hand by an ouraion, a soldier would have no choice but to slice off that hand to stop the poison that would lead to his certain death.

CLAIM TO FRIGHT FAME

So where does a monster like this come from? There are several theories, but according to ancient historian Pierre de Beauvais, the ouraion or basilisk is hatched from an egg—possibly an ordinary chicken egg, but under some unusual circumstances. The egg must first come from an older chicken, be laid outside the nest in foul-smelling mud, and then be hatched by a toad.

THE MOST FEARSOME FANTASY CREATURE

The Manticora

Try to imagine an animal who is a horrifying blend of the worst of all nightmare beasts. This is the manticora. There are over three dozen names for this beast, but they all mean one thing: man-eater!

Begin by picturing a huge body the size of a horse, yet with the form of a vicious red lion. Top this image with a human face, ears, and piercing, ice-blue eyes. When this monster opens his gaping jaws, spectators are astounded by the sight of sinister triple rows of jagged teeth. Continuing down the body is yet another surprise: The tail of the manticora is shaped like that of a giant scorpion, complete with a scorpion's painful sting and deadly venom.

A cluster of poisonous, foot-long spines line the

tail and the manticora can shoot them off like arrows in all directions. But perhaps most chilling is the manticora's voice, said to be a spine-tingling, musical blend of panpipes and trumpet.

In the Middle Ages, the manticora, thought to be the embodiment of evil, was said to live in the depths of the earth. It was also thought, like the werewolf, to be capable of magical and supernatural powers. Even as late as the 1930s, peasants in Spain still considered the manticora a beast of ill omen. A dangerous, cruel, and vicious creature, the manticora has reigned for more than 2,500 years.

CLAIM TO FRIGHT FAME

During the Middle Ages, the manticora was as popular a fantasy beast as the unicorn has been in recent years, but with a very different character! It became the symbol of envy and the embodiment of evil.

Chapter 3

PETRIFYING PEOPLE AND PLACES

hat terrifies you? What makes your blood run cold and causes fear to well up in your chest like a geyser? In most cases, what you don't know about something is really the scariest part. Petrifying people, places, and possessions are real. But be prepared: what you don't know—and possibly will never know—about these stories is likely to keep you up at night.

THE MOST MYSTERIOUS REAL CRIMINAL

Jack the Ripper

Considered the first serial killer, Jack the Ripper terrified London, England, in 1888 and 1889 by killing five women in the poor inner-city neighborhood of Whitechapel. Using a long, sharp knife, he slashed and hacked his victims until they were barely recognizable. These murders came at a time when it was supposedly safe to walk the streets at night. Jack the Ripper changed all that.

The killer left frightening clues such as initials drawn in blood on walls near his victims. But for some reason the

police were never able to tie these clues to a single suspect. The murderer further chilled London by boasting of his crimes in letters, written in red ink, then sent to the newspapers. He signed his name Jack and called himself "The Ripper." After the fifth murder in a four-month period, the killings stopped as abruptly as they had started.

Scotland Yard, London's metropolitan police force famous for its criminal investigation department, tracked a number of possible suspects, including Prince Albert Victor, grandson of Queen Victoria. But they never cracked the case. It took years for the people of London to stop fearing this wretched evildoer who seemed to lurk around every dark corner. Now one hundred-plus years have passed, and it's probably safe to assume that this anonymous killer is no longer a threat!

CLAIM TO FRIGHT FAME

In the early 1980s, a strange diary was found containing intricate details of these murders and offering up the identity of the possible murderer, who was known as an upstanding member of the English community. The most disturbing piece of information was the handwritten admission of Jack the Ripper stating that he cut out the organs of several of his victims, took them home . . . and ate them!

Although the autopsy details were sketchy, there was evidence that several of the victims had, in fact, been missing those oh-so-vital organs and that the person who removed them seemed to have thorough medical knowledge of the body and a skill with surgical tools.

THE SCARIEST AUTHOR

Stephen King

He likes to scare you to death if he can, by going for the jugular. He thinks of himself as a stage manager or puppeteer of evil. He knows where all the trapdoors are that you'll fall into when you devour his pages. His name is Stephen King, and all you have to do is read one of his books to know why he is the world's scariest author!

With more than 200 million books in print and several blockbuster movies, King is the master of fright, the authority on horror. One of the big reasons for his success is that his books appeal to universal fears: fear of death, fear of closed spaces, fear of vampires, inanimate objects gone mad, and the radically gross, such as huge numbers of spiders or rats. King has an impressive ability to elicit fear, terror, and horror in the reader. As he says, "If you're not willing to go for the throat and scare the pants off the reader, you ought not be a horror writer."

So, what is he like as a person? King, for all practical considerations, is just a "normal" guy. As a little boy he was afraid of common things like not being accepted by his friends, monster movies, the dark, ghosts, and the boogeyman. But when he translates those common fears into stories in his own bizarre and twisted fashion, they become blood-curdling works of horror.

King believes that the reason people read horror fiction is because the material is a rehearsal for their own death, and people are fascinated with death. Why does Stephen King write horror fiction? "I've written all these books because I'm havin' a blast," he explains. "That's the same reason I'll keep writing 'em forever!"

Stephen King lives in a 24-room mansion in Bangor, Maine, with his wife, Tabitha, and their children. He says his biggest goal in life is to stay happily married and watch his kids grow up.

Runner-Up: Edgar Allan Poe

The rhythmic th-thump of a heartbeat sounds like thunder in your ears. Your palms are sweating buckets. It's a warm, balmy night, but for some strange reason you feel cold. A shiver skitters up your spine. Could it be you are reading something written by one of the scariest authors of all time . . . Edgar Allan Poe?

Poe is a master of the mysterious, the guru of the gruesome. His short stories are some of the most tormented reading you can get your hands on. Try "The Pit and the Pendulum" or "The Tell-Tale Heart" for starters. His poetry also overflows with haunting images, sad, lonely characters, and thoughts of death. "The Raven," his most well-known work of poetry, has become a creepy classic favorite among horror lovers and English teachers alike.

MOST DANGEROUS PLACE

The Bermuda Triangle

The Bermuda Triangle is a triangular-shaped stretch of bright blue ocean that spans an area in the Atlantic Ocean from the tip of Miami, Florida, to San Juan, Puerto Rico, and to the tiny island of Bermuda. This 140,000-square-mile (364,000 km) stretch of prime ocean has been known to swallow unfortunate voyagers like a python swallowing a pig . . . one gulp at a time!

To date, more than two hundred ships and planes have disappeared in this region without leaving a trace of their existence. Not a single oil slick on the water or stick of damaged debris has surfaced from these missing vessels.

Sailing ships, tankers, yachts, navy bombers, and even rescue planes have all disappeared in the Bermuda Triangle area, with reports noted as recently as 1973.

The most baffling disappearance occurred in 1945, when Flight 19, an entire squadron of five Avenger torpedo bombers, took off from the Fort Lauderdale naval air station on a sunny December afternoon. The squadron, which included a fourteen-member flight crew, had planned a brief, routine practice mission. Instead they vanished, never to be seen again. One of the search planes sent to rescue them also disappeared, a few hours later.

43

It's one thing for a single plane or ship to vanish in rough weather or a freak storm—and even then, there would be some trace. But in the case of Flight 19, there were five individual aircraft, all vanishing at precisely the same moment, and not leaving behind a single hint they had ever existed.

What causes a seemingly normal stretch of ocean to swallow up ships and airplanes, as well as hundreds of passengers? No one knows for sure, but there are plenty of theories. One is that the missing people and their vessels were abducted by aliens from another planet.

Other explanations suggest that the Bermuda Triangle is the location of the lost continent of Atlantis, an ancient civilization of supreme beings. According to legend, the technically advanced people of Atlantis perished when their entire continent sank into the ocean and disappeared. Some psychics believe that the vibrational properties that made Atlantis the superpower it was thought to be may also have contributed to the disappearances.

Scientists have tried for years to unravel the mysteries of the Bermuda Triangle, claiming that the disappearances were the result of freak storms and strong currents. They have employed the highest technology available, including submarines and bathyspheres (underwater space capsules) to examine the area in minute detail. But they still do not know what has caused these amazing disappearances. The dangerous and deadly Bermuda Triangle continues to puzzle researchers, and will likely do so for years to come.

THE FIRST RECORDED HAUNTED HOUSE

The House of Philosopher Athenodorus

The ancient Greeks, who lived in the days before the birth of Jesus Christ, had an active relationship with other worlds, supernatural creatures, and their own dead. The first true haunted-house story ever recorded was adapted from a letter by Pliny the Younger, a well-known historian, to his friend Sura, in which Pliny describes the eerie event. The following account is based on that letter.

There once was a house in Athens, Greece, where dreadful sounds—spine-chilling moans, clanking chains, heavy footsteps, and horrifying shrieks—shattered the still of night. It was rumored that the sounds came from a ghostly old man with a long, tangled beard and a robe that reeked of filth. The ghost was shackled with heavy chains that clanked as he roamed the house.

When seen, the ghost would glare ominously into the observer's eyes and shake his arms furiously. On several occasions, nonbelievers scoffed at the story and offered to spend the night in the house. Within a few hours, however, they'd be terrified beyond their wildest dreams. Furthermore, everyone who visited the house after dark died soon after. As word of this horrifying ghost spread throughout the city, and as bodies turned up as evidence, the house was avoided by everyone.

About fifteen years after the mysterious deaths occurred, a philosopher, Athenodorus, passed the deserted house. He liked its solitude and thought it would be an ideal place in which to think and write about his work. Inquiring about the house, he learned of its dismal reputation, but because of the low rent and quiet surroundings, Athenodorus didn't let the stories worry him.

The philosopher moved into the house at once, and on the first night he decided to do nothing but watch for the dreadful phantom. He watched and watched. The hours passed. Finally, it was so quiet that Athenodorus forgot all about the ghost and began writing. Suddenly he heard the sounds of rattling chains. Looking up from his work, he listened intently. The noise, he realized, was coming closer and closer with every passing minute. The clanking was accompanied by dreadful moans and evil cries. When it  became more than he could bear, he rose from his desk and walked slowly to the door. Gently, he opened the creaky door, and in the dimly lit hallway he saw the very figure that had been described to him.

The ghost fixed blazing eyes on Athenodorus and beckoned him with a long, bony finger. To the utter amazement of the phantom, Athenodorus waved him away and sat down to continue writing! The ghost persisted, shaking his chains and moaning so hideously that it was impossible for the philosopher to work. Athenodorus rose and reached for his lamp, and with that, the thing turned and led him through the decaying, dust-filled corridors. Moaning all the while, the phantom led Athenodorus out into the pitch-black darkness to a dense clump of shrubs. With a final, agonizing moan, the thing vanished into the ground.

The philosopher immediately went to the authorities and described the chilling incident in detail. A team instantly began digging up the dirt where the ghost had disappeared. Several feet beneath the surface they struck something hard. They cleared away the dirt and broke out into a cold sweat at what they saw. It was the remains of a body—skeleton bones chained in shackles so ancient that on exposure to the air they virtually crumbled. The bones were taken and placed in a graveyard. The house in Athens was never again haunted by the miserable phantom.

Runners-Up: Top Five Famous Haunts

1. **The Winchester House, San Francisco, California—** Owned by the family who manufactured the Winchester rifle, the house is said to be haunted by the spirits of thousands of Native Americans killed by the weapon of the white man.

2. **The Borley Rectory, England—**England's most haunted house is thought to be home to a number of apparitions, including two headless ghosts and a phantom nun.

3. **The White House, Washington, D.C.—**It's reported that the ghost of Abraham Lincoln was seen by President Theodore Roosevelt, his wife, Edith, and Queen Wilhelmina of the Netherlands, as well as other guests and various White House staff personnel.

4. **Hannah House, Indianapolis, Indiana—**This 19th-century haunted mansion was once a major link in the Underground Railroad, the escape network that rescued slaves from the South before the Civil War.

5. **Glamis Castle, Scotland—**This old castle boasts three separate apparitions: the spirit of a half-man, half-monster born to the Earl of Strathmore; a grey-haired lady who allegedly poisoned her husband and was burned at the stake for being a witch; and an ex-servant reported to be a vampire, who was bricked up in the walls for her misdeeds.

THE MOST HAUNTED HOSPITAL

Prince Alfred Hospital, Sydney, Australia

Hospitals can be scary enough. But what about a *haunted* hospital? Prince Alfred Hospital in Sydney, Australia, tops this incredible claim to fame with a beautiful ghost nurse who has walked its halls since the mid-1950s.

This anonymous ghostly apparition is apparently as dedicated to her job in the afterlife as she was before her tragic and untimely death. She is thought to be the ghost

of a once dedicated employee of the hospital who contracted tuberculosis with no hope of recovery. She actually died as a result of a fall from a high verandah, but in spite of her injuries, that very night she was back, tending to patients who needed her.

The nurse, called the Good Ghost Sister, has been encountered going into the operating room just before important operations are to be performed. What is she doing there? Checking the instruments? Guiding the hands of the surgeons? Consoling the patients? No one seems to know for sure. While her appearance has caused some stress and confusion among the hospital staff, no one seems to fear her seemingly gentle spirit.

In fact, more often than not, this ghostly night sister has actually saved lives by alerting an on-duty nurse (a living one) to the bedside of patients right before they were to experience a life-threatening crisis.

Runner-Up: Haunted Hospital turned Fraternity House

When the Kansas State University Delta Sigma Phi fraternity moved into the old St. Mary's Hospital building at 1100 Fremont Street in 1974, it took over more than just bricks and plaster. A resident ghost came with the building, a former patient named George Segal.

George was the last person to die in the hospital before it was sold to the fraternity. Apparently, he rolled off his bed in the middle of the night and was trapped between the bed frame and the wall. The hospital staff didn't find George lying on the floor, and the elderly man died shortly after the fall.

The Delta Sigma Phi brothers still hear George in the dead of night. He turns lights on and off, opens locked doors and windows, and uses the third-floor hallway as his own private bowling alley.

THE MOST HAUNTED HOUSE

Amityville

It's been years since a prosperous Italian family was murdered in their home at 112 Ocean Avenue in Amityville, New York. The brutal events that took place on Wednesday, November 13, 1974, at 3:02 A.M. have caused 112 Ocean Avenue—dubbed "Amityville" by the media—to become one of the most feared haunted houses in the world.

51

The crime: Six family members—mother, father, and four children ranging in age from nine to fifteen—were murdered by a .35 caliber rifle. Everyone in the family was killed but one—eldest son Ronnie "Butch" DeFoe, twenty-three years old, who at about 4:00 A.M. got up, shaved, showered, dressed, and went to work seemingly unaware of (or unsympathetic to) the carnage he left behind.

A painstaking investigation followed, and the case became known worldwide. In 1975, Ronnie DeFoe was convicted of killing his family in cold blood and sentenced to twenty-five years to life for each of the six murders.

The house was then purchased by George Lee Lutz and his wife, Katherine, on December 18, 1975. Twenty-eight days after the couple and their three children moved in, the family fled the house in terror. They reported that the house was haunted by evil forces. Katherine said she was repeatedly levitated from the bed, and that whenever she looked into the mirror her face was transformed into that of an aged hag. The children were haunted by spirits that shook them from their beds at night and chased them around the bedroom until they fell exhausted onto the floor. George reported that green slime flowed freely from keyholes and closed doors. When the family brought in a priest to "clear the home of evil forces," a loud male voice ordered him to leave and threatened to kill him. Authorities were skeptical and insisted the entire family take a lie detector test. Each member of the Lutz household passed the polygraph exam.

Experienced researchers continued to question the case, since it appeared that many of the occurrences could have had normal explanations. Those interpretations, however, have never been investigated. Also, because the author of the original Amityville book made a lot of money on his research and writing some people still believe that the Amityville horror is a hoax.

Chapter 4

EERIE ENTERTAINMENT

hile thousands of horror flicks line the video rental store shelves, a few simply jump out of the pack and beg to be seen. The new wave of horror movies competes to see how much blood and gore can be packed into each minute.

But the old movies, while lacking the sophisticated special-effects techniques of today, offered up their own brand of horror. These oldies, masters of the nail-biting, hide-your-eyes, spooky horror genre, didn't depend on gallons of blood but relied on the real, horrifying payoffs of excellent storytelling. The best of them, detailed here, are not to be missed.

THE FIRST HORROR MOVIE

The Cabinet of Dr. Caligari

The very first horror movie set the stage for many to follow. *The Cabinet of Dr. Caligari* is a black-and-white silent film made in 1919. Even though it uses title cards instead of spoken dialogue, the mood created by this movie is scary enough to make it one of the all-time classics, according to all the major movie historians.

Shot in Germany immediately after World War I, *The Cabinet of Dr. Caligari* redefined the rules for movies of the time. Most movies made during this era tried to look as real as possible, but *Dr. Caligari* changed that. Rather than use actual locations, the director set out to make the unreal look real. Every set and backdrop was meticulously

designed and painted by hand. The distinct style featured sharp, jagged forms and buildings with pointed roofs. The backdrops are close and threatening, giving the feeling that the buildings could swallow up the people who live there. The final film was tinted in green, brown, and cold blue.

In the movie, Dr. Caligari comes to a German town with his carnival exhibit: a wooden cabinet containing a strange, pale man who sleeps nearly all the time. The man who walks in his sleep is more than a little frightening. Only Dr. Caligari can awaken the sleeping man, whom he claims can predict the future. Caligari challenges the audience to ask a question. A bold man in the audience asks (through subtitles), "How long will I live?"

The sleepwalker answers, "Only until dawn!"

The people viewing the carnival laugh uproariously. Surely this is a joke! But while the bold man sleeps in his bed that night, a shadowy figure creeps into his room and kills him with a very long knife. And he becomes the first of many to die.

CLAIM TO FRIGHT FAME

The Cabinet of Dr. Caligari, the first film ever made that was not based on a true story or on a book, was written directly for the screen by Hans Janowitz and Carl Mayer. It was also the first film that purposely tried to look strange and unreal. It is dark and moody, representing an inner fear far more terrifying than something easily recognized. The characters' odd, jerky, and inhuman movements add to the film's nightmarish feeling.

THE SPOOKIEST MOVIE

Halloween

The setting could be Anytown, U.S.A. It could even be the street where you live. And therein lies the seed of fear that will send you scrambling for the locks on your doors and windows. Just a hint: If you're getting ready to baby-sit, don't rent this movie. Baby-sitters are a favorite target of the killer in *Halloween* (1978).

It was the first and will probably remain the best slasher film ever made. The killer, named Michael, is not supernatural. He's flesh and blood. He bleeds when stabbed and can be stopped by bullets—and yet he, like Jason, obstinately refuses to die.

By using the camera as the eyes of the murderer, viewers are treated to a front-row seat to horror. The murderer is

revealed slowly: the tip of his shoe . . . his hand dangling an oversized knife . . . his breathing so loud it sounds as if he's right outside. And then he strikes, slashing and gashing everything in his path.

This was the first commercial success for director John Carpenter, who also co-wrote the script and composed the skin-crawling musical score. It was also the first movie role for actress Jamie Lee Curtis, who plays the good-girl baby-sitter, spending nearly the full ninety-three minutes trying not to become pumpkin pulp as the nightmarish slasher slaughters everyone around her.

CLAIM TO FRIGHT FAME

Halloween was thought to be full of buckets of blood and gore, and yet when it was edited to be shown on network television, where gory, bloody scenes are not allowed, the editors had to remove only a brief, tight twenty-two seconds. This is because John Carpenter used unusual scare tactics that made you think what you watched was worse than it really was. Look for Michael, also called the Shape, in *Halloween II* (1981); *Halloween III: Season of the Witch* (1983); *Halloween 4: The Return of Michael Myers* (1987); and finally, *Halloween 5* (1989).

57

THE BEST MOVIE TO WATCH IN THE DARK . . . ALONE!

Dead of Night

Dead of Night (1945) intertwines *five* supernatural tales and manages to string them together so as to bring you slowly to the peak of terror. By the time you realize how truly frightening this movie is, you will be too scared to get up and turn it off.

The movie starts with a man receiving a phone call to come to Pilgrim's Farm, a Victorian country house. As he pulls up in his car, he senses something strangely familiar about this place.

Once inside, he meets several people who seem very pleas- ant, but he soon realizes they are characters in a recurring nightmare that has been tormenting him for a long time.

One by one the guests tell of their own terrifying encounters with the supernatural, in bloodcurdling detail. One

describes how he purposely misses a bus, only to find the bus later crashes. Another dreams of consoling a crying child, and then discovers that the child has been dead for years. The third story is the tale of a woman who buys a valuable Victorian mirror for her fiancé. The mirror is haunted, with a history of madness and murder. In the next tale, a golfer tricks his buddy into committing suicide. And in the fifth and most chilling tale, a ventriloquist believes his dummy is plotting against him. As the stories come alive, real life turns into insanity and murder—only to end with the man receiving a phone call—and the whole nightmare begins again.

In order to give this picture a special look, the producers commissioned four different directors, each with his own special film style.

FIVE THINGS TO DO BEFORE WATCHING A SCARY MOVIE ALONE:

1. Lock all the doors.
2. Close all the curtains.
3. Turn on some lights.
4. Move the phone near you.
5. Have a friend's phone number handy, just in case.

THE MOST WICKED WEREWOLF MOVIE

The Wolf Man

"Even a man who is pure in heart and says his prayers at night, may become a wolf when the wolf-bane blooms and the autumn moon is bright."

An old gypsy folk rhyme told in the beginning of *The Wolf Man* (1941) predicts only a sliver of the terror that ultimately unfolds. It's the chilling transformation of a hopeful young man into a savage, bloodthirsty beast of the night.

The Wolf Man is the vehicle that thrust Lon Chaney, Jr., into the spotlight as one of the premier horror actors of all time. But Chaney did not accomplish this feat alone.

The look of this creature was created by makeup man Jack Pierce, who also created the face of the monster in *Frankenstein,* as played by Boris Karloff.

CLAIM TO FRIGHT FAME

Even though Chaney never actually resembled a real wolf, the effect of his makeup was so chilling that it set the standard for what all movie wolfmen looked like for years to come.

By applying yak hairs *one at a time* to Chaney's face, Pierce brought to life this terrible being. The makeup process was so time-consuming and tedious that it took an entire day to shoot a single fifteen-second transformation from man to wolf.

Although many werewolf movies have been made, *The Wolf Man* stands as the first and the scariest to date.

THE SCARIEST RADIO SHOW

The War of the Worlds

A single, one-hour radio broadcast plunged the United States into panic when more than a million people across the nation heard that Martians—aliens from the planet Mars— had invaded earth!

It was a calm Sunday night on October 30, 1938. A little-known but extremely talented actor, Orson Welles, was the producer, director, and principal actor for a popular CBS radio show, called *Mercury Theater*. Wanting to put a little punch into his radio show and add to the scary theme of Halloween, Welles prepared a radio drama of the H.G. Wells novella *The War of the Worlds*. The story was a dramatic fictional tale of aliens invading the planet and ultimately destroying it.

The radio broadcast began innocently with a Latin dance band playing some up-beat music. The music was abruptly interrupted by a series of chilling news reports detailing "a huge, flaming object" that had fallen on a farm in Grover's Mill, New Jersey. As the broadcast continued, the news reports became more and more ominous, describing "aliens as tall as skyscrapers" taking over New York City!

The one million listeners swelled to over six million in a matter of minutes. People who tuned in later had no idea the broadcast was only a radio play—they thought it was real! Even residents of Grover's Mill were preparing for the invasion.

A Pittsburgh housewife tried unsuccessfully to poison herself because she didn't want to die at the hands of Martians. Hysterical mobs stormed the streets, looking to fend off Martians with their bare hands. Those who had guns in their homes loaded them and sat waiting for the attacks to begin. Hundreds of people phoned the newspapers and radio stations. The nation was nearly paralyzed with fear.

Finally, at the end of the hour, the broadcast was over, and those who were still listening learned the truth. Others had turned their radios off and were preparing for the invasion. It took days to convince those unsuspecting listeners who'd left their radios in the middle of the broadcast that this had been simply a heightened way to celebrate Halloween.

Chapter 5

CURSES, SUPERSTITIONS, AND DEADLY GAMES

People did not first become frightened or scared out of their minds from creepy horror books or films. Terrifying things have been happening since time began—from weird superstitions to unbelievably spooky legends. Let's just hope that in the case of these howl-of-fame entries, history does not repeat itself!

THE MOST TERRIFYING SUPERSTITION IN HISTORY

The Evil Eye

If you are superstitious, you probably avoid black cats, ladders, and the number 13. But there is an even more frightening superstition lurking in the minds of some—the evil eye. No superstitions have aroused more fear and dread throughout history than the evil eye. This is the belief that some people possess the power to bring bad luck to others by looking at them.

Fear of the evil eye's terrifying powers dates back to Biblical times, when it was thought that anyone whose eyes were an unusual color, narrow or widely set, of a size or shape that didn't seem to fit the face, or even slightly crossed could be accused of possessing the ability to zap people. One look was thought to cause misfortunes of every kind—even death!

During the Middle Ages, those persons even suspected of casting the evil eye were publicly tried as witches and destroyed. Nearly every culture has feared some version of the evil eye and has developed a way of warding off its destructive effects.

In Italy, wearing nine grains of salt in a sachet around your neck

65

or carrying a piece of iron, a key, or a horseshoe would give you sufficient protection.

In England, painting or tattooing the symbol of the eye on your body would keep you safe.

American folklore suggested wearing red ribbons or painting a red spot on your forehead for effective prevention.

The Jewish tradition recommended spitting on your right shoe before putting it on, or spitting over your left shoulder.

In Spain and Portugal, wearing sprigs of sage or rosemary was thought to prevent an evil spell.

For protection from the evil eye, the ancient Greeks wore the amulet of Medusa (see page 32).

Runner-Up: The Number Thirteen

The number thirteen has many superstitions attached to it. For one thing, it is believed that if thirteen people sit around a table at the same time, one of them will die before one year has passed. The genesis of this notion is thought to date back to Biblical times and the Last Supper, when Jesus Christ dined along with his twelve disciples before being killed. Thirteen is also thought to be the correct number for a coven of witches.

Because of this numeric superstition, many hotels and tall buildings that have more than thirteen floors skip the number thirteen, going straight from twelve to fourteen.

THE MOST CHILLING CURSE ON A TOMB

The Curse of King Tutankhamen's Tomb

One of the wealthiest kings of ancient Egypt died as a young man, not quite twenty years old. His grave, or tomb, within a giant pyramid, was buried beneath thousands of layers of sand. The burial chamber inside contained not only King Tutankhamen, but his entire, vast earthly fortune of magnificent statues and works of art made from solid gold—a collection worth millions of dollars. This burial site remained sealed and hidden from grave robbers for over 3,000 years—until a day in November 1922, when British archaeologist

Howard Carter stumbled upon a secret, well-hidden door. It was a passageway into spectacular splendor.

Engraved above the door to Tut's tomb were these words of warning:

DEATH SHALL COME ON SWIFT WINGS
TO THOSE WHO DISTURB
THE SLEEP OF THE PHARAOH

But, the diggers didn't heed the warning.

After at least twenty-two people associated with the discovery and excavation of King Tutankhamen's tomb died under

CLAIM TO FRIGHT FAME

Three weird, unexplained occurrences related to the death of Lord Carnarvon help to reinforce the Tutankhamen cursed-tomb theory.

The first is that at the exact moment that Lord Carnarvon died in an Egyptian hotel room, his dog in England suddenly howled terribly and himself died.

The second unexplainable occurrence is that at the exact moment of Carnarvon's death, the lights in his hotel room suddenly went out, as well as the lights of the entire city of Cairo, Egypt. No technical explanation was ever given for the power failure, although a full investigation was made.

And finally, the mosquito bite that killed Carnarvon was on his left cheek. When the remains of the boy king were examined, doctors noted a small scab on his left cheek—in the exact same place as Lord Carnarvon's fatal insect bite.

strange and suspicious circumstances within six years after the opening of the tomb, some came to believe those words to be a curse.

Lord Carnarvon, the financial sponsor of the expedition and one of the few on hand when the tomb was actually unsealed, died five months after the tomb was opened. The cause of death was listed as a fever from an infected mosquito bite. But newspaper headlines shrieked it was the fault of the curse. Within days, the next in line was Georges Bénédite, the head of the Department of Egyptian Antiquities at the Louvre Museum in Paris. His death was due to a stroke. The son of Lord Westbury, Carter's former secretary, was found dead in his bed, though no cause of death was ever determined. After that, his father jumped to his death from his seventh floor London apartment.

MOST DEADLY CURSE ON THE RICH AND FAMOUS

Rudolph Valentino's Ring

Rudolph Valentino, a gifted actor with intense, hypnotic eyes, was one of the most popular young hunks of the 1920s. Dashing and sophisticated, he embodied the essence of the romantic hero, but at the height of his career in 1926, Valentino died of a gastric ulcer. There are reports, however, that his death had more to do with an unusual piece of jewelry than a usually curable medical condition.

In early 1926, a famous psychic named Chaw Mank spent an afternoon with the legendary film star, who was his old friend. During their conversation, Mank noticed a strange new cat's-eye ring on Valentino's finger and commented on it. Valentino slipped the ring off his finger and handed it to Mank, telling how he'd bought it in San Francisco's Chinatown. The old shopkeeper had called it a destiny ring.

Valentino narrowed his powerful gaze and playfully asked his friend, "What do you see as my destiny?"

Mank, the psychic, reported that a powerful vision and sense of dread hit him like a thunderbolt. At once he saw his friend in the throes of a violent and painful death. Shaking off the distressing feelings with a shudder, Mank simply smiled and agreed with Valentino that the ring ought to be lucky. Not long after this encounter, Valentino was stricken

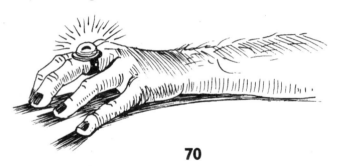

by the ulcer. He was wearing the destiny ring on the hot August day when he died.

But the legend doesn't stop there. A few years later a popular singer named Russ Columbo was cast to play Valentino in a movie about the star's life. He was given the ring and told to learn to impersonate the great movie star. Chaw Mank warned Columbo that the ring carried a dangerous curse and told him not to wear it. But Columbo brushed off Mank's concerns. Russ Columbo was killed in an automobile accident soon after, just a few days before he was to begin filming the movie of Valentino's life.

The ring then passed to a close friend of Columbo's, Joe Casino, who treated the cursed piece of jewelry with a little more respect. Casino placed it in a display case and promised not to wear it until the curse had worn off. The destiny ring lay on display for several years, until Casino decided it was safe to wear it. A few days after this fateful decision, Casino was struck and killed by a truck!

CLAIM TO FRIGHT FAME

Valentino's ring of death, though not a valuable piece of jewelry unto itself, became an object surrounded with mystery. A New York radio station acquired the ring to give away to the person who could write the best letter on the tragic properties of the strange cat's-eye bauble.

A barber won the contest and the ring, but this is where the story ends. There is no information as to whether the curse continued, or whether it was confined to only those people associated with Valentino and Columbo.

THE MOST DEADLY GAME

Aztec Ball Game

How would you feel about playing a game where if you lost, you would be killed?

The Olmecs, a highly developed Meso-American Indian culture who created an advanced civilization throughout the highlands of Mexico from 1500 to 600 B.C., played exactly this kind of game. According to archaeologists, this ball game was even more popular than football games are today!

The ball court was shaped like the letter "H," with the crossbar of the "H" being as long as 200 feet—one third shorter than a football field. The ball was round and made

from a heavy rubber substance. The trick was that the players could never hit the ball with their hands or their feet, and the ball could never touch the ground. Players kept the ball in the air at all times by bouncing it off their hips, knees, elbows, and possibly their heads.

We don't know how the game was scored, but pictures, called friezes, carved into stone walls clearly show how each game ended—with one entire team beheaded as a sacrifice to the gods. Most archaeologists assume that it was the losing team who lost their lives. But we don't know for sure: The winners might have "won" the great honor of being sent to play ball in the big league with the gods.

Runner-Up: The Gladiator Games

The professional fighters of ancient Rome, around 200 B.C., were the hottest ticket in town. "Gladiator games," as they called them, were held in arenas known as amphitheaters. Thousands of spectators would crowd together to watch the gladiators go at each other with swords, spears, spiked balls on chains, and various other weapons.

Usually the fight would pit a smaller man with few weapons against a larger, heavily armed man. The gladiators were ordered by the Roman emperors to fight to the death. But if one man was able to defeat the other by disarming him without mortally wounding him, the crowd could decide if the loser lived or died. If the crowd waved handkerchiefs, he was allowed to live. If they made a hand gesture with the thumb pointing down, the man had to die!

THE MOST LETHAL LEGEND

The Poison Damsel

The poison damsel was invented long before there were any guns or weapons. She was considered to be a tribe's most secret, human weapon. This was one effective—and demented—way to get back at enemies.

According to an ancient legend, a tribe would choose their most beautiful female baby to be their poison damsel. Her appearance was of utmost importance, as the success of the weapon depended on the girl growing up to be gorgeous

and irresistible. The baby was taken from her parents and raised in a pit with the most poisonous snakes, spiders, scorpions, and naturally toxic shrubs and herbs. The baby was given small doses of the various poisons on a daily basis. The doses would be so small that she would not die, but would instead begin to absorb the poisons into her system. As she grew, she would thus be immune to these poisons, but would become poisonous herself. At least, that's the way the story went. A mere kiss, scratch, or bite from a poison damsel was supposedly enough to inflict the poison into her victim, killing him or her instantly.

Once the girl grew up and was properly armed with her poisons, she would be sent into the camp of the enemy to inflict her deadly damage. Before anyone could suspect that this beautiful, innocent young stranger was treacherous and deadly, everyone in the tribe would be infected.

Runner-Up: The Legend of the Greedy Guest

A mysterious tribe in the jungles of Borneo had a reputation for giving lavish gifts of gold ornaments and silk clothing to unsuspecting travellers who lost their way. But these gifts were not given to just anyone. The tribe had an unusual way of telling a worthy traveller from a greedy one. They would place the traveller in their smallest and most humble hut. Instead of water, they would offer him blood to drink, and instead of rice they would feed him worms. He was given only a banana leaf to sleep on instead of a mat. If the traveller was gracious and thanked the tribe for their trouble (despite the disgusting nature of their hospitality), he would be given a large, hollowed-out section of bamboo filled with treasures. If the traveller complained, he'd be given a bamboo log filled with live scorpions that would sting him to a painful death.

THE MOST GHASTLY
URBAN LEGEND

The Graveyard Wager

Like a nasty cold in winter, a good scary story spreads quickly—from friend to friend, from generation to generation, even from culture to culture. An urban legend (which has nothing to do with a city) is actually a tale that has been related over and over again with all kinds of variations, depending on where in the world the story is being told. Though the tale itself may vary, one thing remains the same: The story is thought to be true. Here is one of the most widespread and spooky graveyard accounts ever reported.

Several teenage girls were sleeping over at one friend's home while her parents were out of town. It had been a fun evening spent eating ice cream, dancing, and gossiping about anyone who wasn't present. At midnight, the lights went out and one girl began telling a story she had heard as true.

"An old man was recently buried in the cemetery in the middle of town. There's a rumor going around that he was buried alive. People passing by have heard him trying to claw his way out," the girl declared.

The youngest girl at the sleep-over laughed at the story, so the others dared her to ride her bike the two miles to the

CLAIM TO FRIGHT FAME

Variations of this story have been told around the world for hundreds of years. Many people report that they grew up hearing this exact same story from others who knew the tale to be true! Other folks remember hearing different versions. In some of these, a soldier bets that he has the courage to remain overnight in a cemetery, but he dies from fright after plunging his sword through his long cloak. In others, a drunken man drives his dagger through the hem of his overcoat. Sometimes the person visiting the grave is told to drive a nail into a wooden cross, and the nail goes through part of his clothing.

This incident at the graveyard was even the inspiration for an episode of the television series *Twilight Zone*, where a man was found dead beside a grave, his knife stuck in his coat.

graveyard where the man was buried and prove the story wrong. As proof that she had been there, she was to drive a kitchen knife into the earth below the tombstone.

The young girl was frightened, but too proud not to take the older girls' dare. After she left, the girls crawled into their sleeping bags and waited, wide awake, for her return.

One hour passed and then another, without any sign of their friend. The girls lay awake, terrified that something horrible had happened. They discussed going out that night to look for the girl, but when the oldest girl admitted that she was much too scared to go without an adult, the others agreed. When the sun finally rose, their friend still had not returned. The girls quickly dressed and walked to the grave-yard, each silently praying for their friend's safe return.

They found her almost at once . . . lying dead on top of the man's grave. And as they stood there, petrified, they saw what had happened. The night before, when the young girl had squatted down to push the knife into the dirt, she had unknowingly driven the knife into the hem of her skirt. When she tried to stand up and couldn't, she assumed that the dead man was reaching up through the earth and grab-bing her clothing. Within seconds, the girl died . . . of fright.

THE BIGGEST FRIGHT IN LIFE

Being Buried Alive

Can you imagine anything worse? You fall ill and become so lethargic that your heart rate plummets and your pulse barely registers. A physician incorrectly pronounces you dead, and you're placed in the ground . . . alive! In early America, during the days of unexplored territory and westward-bound pioneers, the technology for assessing life was limited to the stethoscope and a doctor's intuition. And there were quite a

few medical cases in which a person showed no apparent signs of life and was pronounced dead . . . only to be revived later.

In 1865, the disease called cholera swept through a small Wisconsin farm town, and five-year-old Maxie Hoffman caught it. The doctor looked in on him, but he knew that few children recovered from the disease.

Maxie died three days after getting sick, and his small body was placed in a pine coffin with silver handles. On the night following his burial, Maxie's mother awoke wild-eyed, screaming in panic. "I had a dream. Maxie was in his coffin," she told her husband. "He was alive and trying to get out! His hands were under his right cheek. He was twisted. We must go to him!"

Mr. Hoffman reluctantly agreed to her pleadings and gathered a crew together to exhume the body. It was well past one o'clock in the morning when they raised the coffin from the earth. A gasp arose from everyone's lips when they saw Maxie's body. It was twisted to the right side, and his hand was clenched under his cheek—just as his mother had dreamed!

The couple raced their son to the doctor, who detected a faint heartbeat and noticed an unusual warmth to his body. Within the week, Maxie was fully recovered and very much alive!

CLAIM TO FRIGHT FAME

What became of Maxie Hoffman? He lived to the age of eighty-five and died peacefully in Clinton, Iowa. The silver handles from his "first" coffin always held a place of prominence in Maxie's home.

THE MOST GROTESQUE BURIAL RITUAL

Smoking of the Corpses

In a remote jungle on the island of New Guinea, lived a secret tribe of cannibals called the Kukukukus. There was no more vicious and deadly group of people alive. While these cannibals may have survived on potatoes, roots, nuts, and fruit, they also were known to eat people!

Striking at dawn, a band of Kukukukus would destroy an entire village, leaving no living thing behind. Their bloodthirsty ways were infamous and struck such fear into neighboring villages, that even the sight of four or five Kukukukus sent an entire community fleeing in terror.

What the Kukukukus killed they ate. But what did they do when one of their own died? It is a bizarre burial ritual that was practiced as late as 1986, and may still be done today.

The family of the dead person prepared the family hut for the burial ceremony. A small fire was built, over which was placed a raised bamboo platform. The dead body was positioned on the

81

platform in a sitting position, arms and legs lashed to bamboo poles. The family acted as if the dead person were still alive. They placed food in the mouth on a daily basis and even slept in the hut with the body every night. The fire was kept going for six to ten weeks, until the flesh tightened and the corpse shrank to a leathery mass only half its original weight.

When the smoking was complete, the family carried the corpse to a special mountaintop, nearly impossible to reach. There the corpse was propped up on a platform next to other mummified tribe members, where it remained until the birds, ants, and caterpillars ate it from the inside out.

Chapter 6

SINISTER SCIENCE AND NIGHTMARES OF NATURE

Creepy deadly insects, slimy poisonous snakes, and vicious animals . . . they terrify us all. Why? Because they are killers.

These sinister creatures of science and nature can make your blood run cold with fear. Don't take the following entries lightly. One of the chilling living things in this chapter may one day take YOU by surprise!

MOST SINISTER SPIDER

The Black Widow

There's something sickening about the thought of an eight-legged arachnid crawling quickly into your clothes and nesting against the warmth of your skin. And when that creature is a poisonous one like the vicious black widow, the thought is truly paralyzing!

She's about an inch long and shiny black, with a blood-red hourglass-shaped design on her stomach. She hides in any pitch-black location, but seems to prefer trash and the insides of abandoned tires and she lays several masses of eggs during the summer. Each female lives for more than a year and a half! Watch where you step, because if she happens to attack you, she'll make small punctures in your skin and suck out about a tablespoon of blood. At the very least, the bite will cause you severe pain, nausea, and mild paralysis. At worst, the bite will cause a painful death, even to humans.

The male species of the spider (which is about one-quarter the size of the female) is rarely seen, because the female kills and eats him immediately after mating—that's how the black widow got her name!

Black widow spiders are found only in the United States, in almost every region of the country. Sweet dreams!

Runner Up: The Funnel-Web Spider

The Australian funnel-web spider can be found in tropical rainforests of northeastern Australia. The climate is hot and damp, so to keep cool, the funnel-web spider lives in an underground burrow with an entrance shaped like a funnel. It lines the burrow with a silken web, and in the dead of night it emerges to seize small animals, insects, and other prey. It injects poison into its victims through its fangs. The extremely deadly funnel-web is one of the few spiders that can kill people.

THE MOST MENACING MAMMAL

The Vampire Bat

When we think of bats, we usually associate them with dark caves on an eerie Halloween night. But think again! Vampire bats may spend their days in dark retreats like caves, tunnels, and abandoned buildings, but when the sun goes down, they could show up anywhere!

Blood is the vampire bat's only food. In a typical attack the bat lands near his victim, scuttles close, and then leaps onto the body. With its two razor-sharp, triangular front upper teeth, it scoops out a shallow channel in the skin and laps up the blood from the lower end of the channel. Sound gross and intensely painful? Well, it's not. The bat's teeth are so sharp that the bite is generally painless, and the loss of blood isn't significant enough to warrant a transfusion.

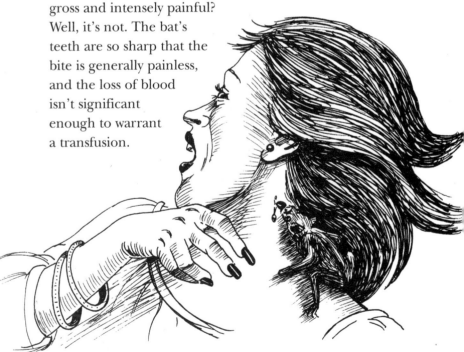

CLAIM TO FRIGHT FAME

The throats of vampire bats are too small to swallow solid particles of food, which is why they live on blood. Scientists believe the saliva of vampire bats contains an anticoagulant, which keeps the blood flowing even after the bat has eaten its dinner. The victim will continue bleeding a little longer, before the blood naturally coagulates, stopping the flow. Greedy to a fault, the vampire bat will lap up large quantities of blood until its body is nearly round and then will clumsily flutter its wings and head for the cave to sleep it off.

Nonetheless, rabies and other fatal diseases may be transmitted from the bat to the victim, causing death if left untreated.

The common vampire bat can be found anywhere from northern Mexico to central Chile and central Argentina. The white-winged vampire bat and the hairy-legged vampire bat exist only in tropical regions. About the size of a small sparrow, they all move as fast as lightning when they're ready to attack, swooping down from the pitch-black sky.

MOST DANGEROUS EXTINCT ANIMAL

Tyrannosaurus Rex

When large, carnivorous dinosaurs ruled the earth, there was plenty of bloodshed, and when a hungry Tyrannosaurus Rex showed his menacing face, every dinosaur in the land knew its days were numbered.

The most famous of all dinosaurs, the T-Rex was the creature that all other dinosaurs feared most. A fully grown Tyrannosaurus Rex was the meanest, most terrifying animal that lived during the Cretaceous Period. Measuring forty-seven feet (14m) long, it was taller than a double-decker bus, and had a skull that alone was more than four feet (1.2m) long.

The T-Rex was armed with a deadly mouth that carried huge, pointed teeth up to six inches (15cm) long!

This enormous flesh-eating animal would charge down on its prey over short distances at a speed of eighteen miles (29 km) per hour. When it captured its victims, it would use deadly strength to throw them onto the ground, after which it would immediately rip into the flesh with its razor-sharp teeth. At the end of its meal, only bones would remain.

Runner-Up: Allosaurus

Although we don't hear much about this type of dinosaur, the Allosaurus was also a deadly killer. Its body was incredibly strong, weighing in at over two tons. More than seventy curved, saw-edged teeth lined its jaws. Pointing backwards, these teeth forced chunks of meat into its hungry, gaping mouth. This wide-mouthed meat-eater would attack anything in sight. Only the dreaded T-Rex gave the Allosaurus pause. The thrill for the Allosaurus seemed to lie as much in the attack as in the meal.

THE MOST VENOMOUS VIPER

King Cobra

Mention the words *poisonous snake* to most people, and a chill starts in their nervous system and slowly spreads up the spine. There, it bubbles up to the nape of the neck, to resolve itself into a slimy sweat. Prepare to read about the deadliest snake of all time.

If you ever find yourself walking through the woods and you happen to hear an angry, deep, resonant hiss similar to the growl of a small dog, watch your step! That's the sound that the king cobra makes just prior to a deadly attack. And king cobras have been known to bite innocent victims, even when they haven't been provoked.

This scary species attains a length of eighteen feet (5.5m) and is considered the world's most dangerous snake. It is found year-round in abundance in southeast Asia and India, particularly at the tip of India near the Arabian Sea. The head of a king cobra is short and flattened, and its body is slender. To frighten off an enemy, the cobra hisses, raises the front of its body, and spreads out the skin around its neck to form a hood. Although most king cobras slither around on the ground, some can also be found hanging high above your head in a tree, or lurking just beneath the surface of the water in a pond or lake. Should you run across one that is either injured, protecting a nest, or cornered by you or another animal, a vicious attack is imminent. These snakes move at lightning speed when they dive in for an attack. The bite takes less than a second, but the amount of poison they can inject in that time is deadly! A cobra bite can kill an elephant in four hours and a person in just fifteen minutes. The venom that a king cobra carries is toxic to almost every mammal in the animal kingdom.

Runner-Up: Fer-de-lance

Found in Central America, the fer-de-lance is one of the most aggressive snakes on earth. It strikes at lightning speed, and when it injects its prey with a paralyzing venom, there is no hope for survival. What's worse is that the patterns on the snake's skin blend into leaf litter on the forest floor, making the creature impossible to see.

THE MOST FRIGHTENING FISH

Piranha

We all know that wet, weird, and slimy creatures lurk beneath the water. It's all too common to get the willies while standing waist-deep in a swimming hole—if something just happens to slip silently past your legs! But beware if you're in the fresh water of South America, because a deadly fish may be waiting to attack your flesh.

The dreaded freshwater flesh-eating piranha has a well-deserved reputation as a vicious carnivore. This swift swimmer travels in large groups in the Amazon River and will attack any creature in the water, no matter how big. It's been known to kill horses and people! Should you venture into the water sporting a cut or scrape, be prepared to fend off an attack, since piranhas are highly attracted to the scent of blood.

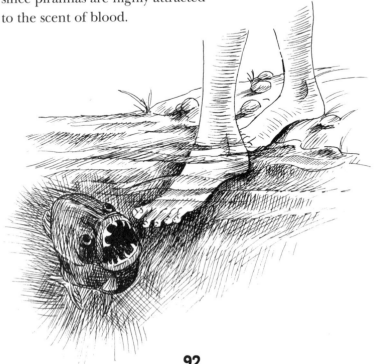

Reaching a length of about two feet (.6m), a sinister size for a killer fish, they are either silver and orange or completely black. They all have deep bodies, saw-edge bellies, and large, blunt heads with superstrong jaws and triangular, razor-sharp teeth that close in a scissorlike bite. Because of their incredibly strong bite, they are able to reduce even a large animal to a skeleton in a matter of minutes. Once they attack, the victim rarely has a prayer of making it out of the water alive!

Runner-Up: The Great White Shark

Great White Sharks are powerful and primitive creatures charging from the depths of the ocean to attack their prey with amazing efficiency. Few animals have created more hysteria than Great Whites. They are rightly feared, for their power and size are extraordinary.

The bizarre thing about Great White attacks on people is that most of the victims survive. Given the immense strength and large teeth of the species, a Great White could instantly kill its victim if it chooses. It usually, however, just bites off an arm or a leg. Popular theory has it that the shark then realizes the human body part is not its usual dinner and swims off for tastier prey.

THE MOST TERRIFYING MONSTER IN THE WORLD

The Monster Under Your Bed

What scares the living daylights out of you? Does the scariest thing in the world live in your imagination? Do the deep, dark corners of your mind harbor unspeakable nightmares? Do you hear unusual noises in the night that make your blood run cold?

Don't feel bad—everyone has his or her own unique idea of the spookiest, scariest thing that could be lurking under the bed.

What's the most terrifying monster in the world? Here's what some boys and girls said while trick-or-treating one very scary Halloween night as they described the monsters that live under their beds:

"It's a monster with gooey stuff all over his face, and he attacks people in the middle of the night." —Nicholas, age 9

"A skeleton with razor-sharp teeth, only one eye, and a super-long tongue. He has a wicked laugh and he carries a butcher knife." —Brett, age 11

"She's a witch with long fingers that she uses to choke the bad kids. She has solid black beady eyes and rotten teeth." —Sarah, age 8

"It's a big blob that opens his mouth as big as a house and eats you when you're not looking." —Rebecca, age 8

"He has a long chin and a high forehead, but no nose or mouth. He has a hundred eyes all over his head and body, so he can see you in the dark. When he calls you by name, you have to go to him, and then . . . you're in trouble." —Casey, age 12

"At first I think she is a good witch that has come to help me fall asleep because she's so beautiful. Then she smiles, and her face turns mean and ugly. She has teeth like a vampire." —Wendy, age 9

Sound silly? Well, when you crawl into bed tonight, you might check *under* the bed first—if you dare . . .

INDEX